Written by Rosie Greening.
Illustrated by Stuart Lynch.

Reindeer of the year!

Rosie Greening · Stuart Lynch

make
believe
ideas

"Today's the day!" says **Santa**, and the **elves** all give a **cheer**.

COMET

Dancer

I ♥ Blitzen

"It's time to find out **WHO** will be . . .

the **REINDEER** of the **YEAR!**"

Every year, this CONTEST
puts the REINDEER to the test.

They each compete to win the prize
and prove they are the best!

The stadium is **buzzing.**

It's **almost** time to **start.**

The nervous **REINDEER** wait backstage, excited to take part!

APPLAUSE!

Dancer

CUPID

COMET

I ♥ BLITZ

First on stage is **Dasher,** who's the **fastest** of the group. She flies round at **turbo speed**

HI MUM!

and does a loop-the-loop.

Reindeer two is COMET,

whose fireworks crack and fizz.

He sets off zooming rockets

that go POP and BANG

and WhiZZ!

And when he does the

snowman STOMP,

the little elves join in!

Reindeer four is

Cupid –

the Singing superstar!

He croons into the microphone and strums on his guitar.

Next up are the reindeer twins: performers five and six.

BLITZEN flips

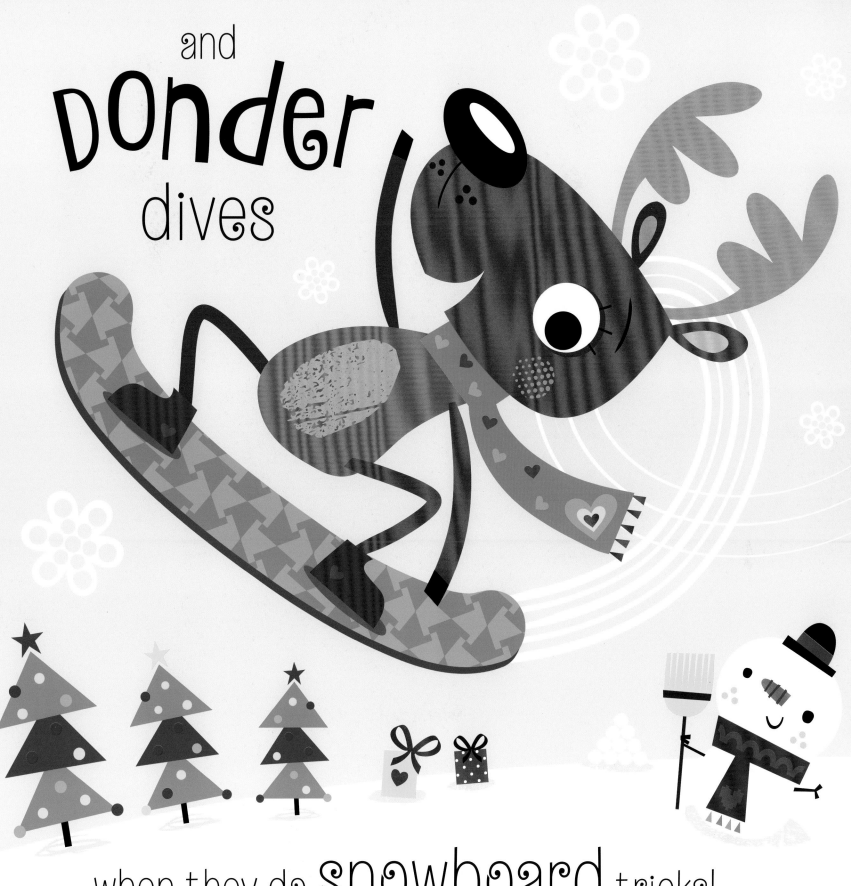

and **DONder** dives

when they do **snowboard** tricks!

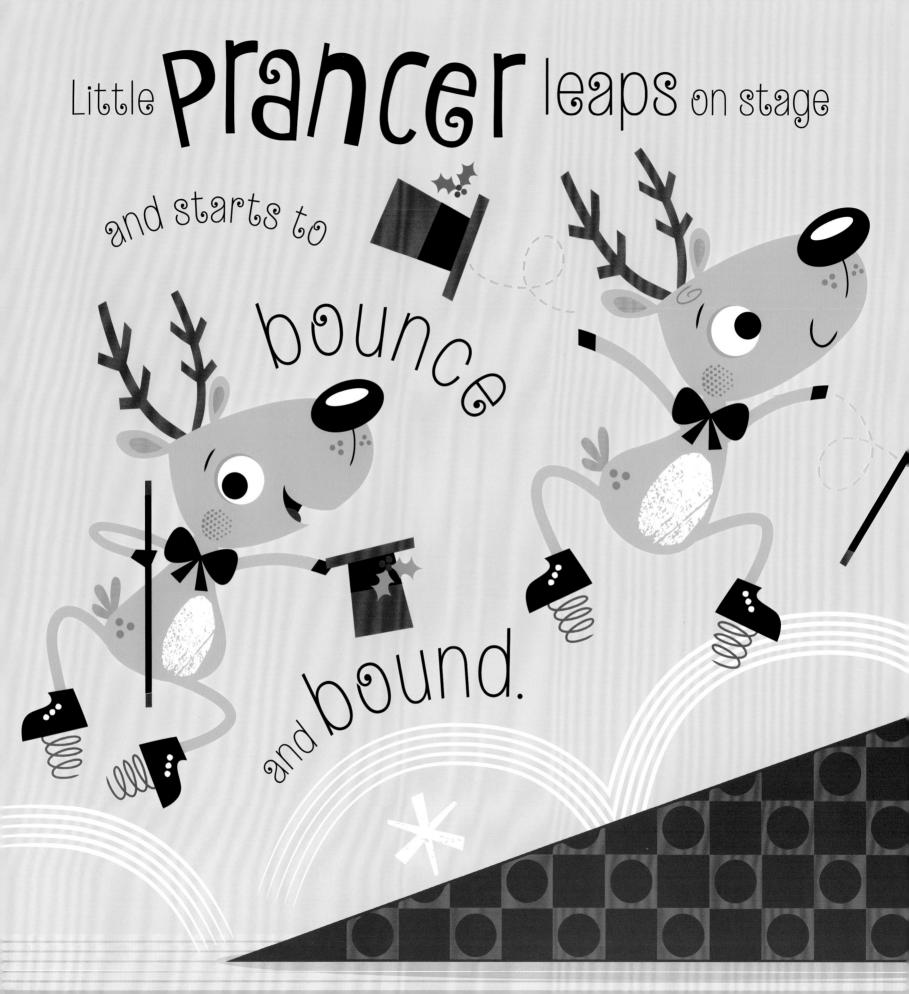

Little **Prancer** leaps on stage

and starts to

bounce

and **bound.**

When it comes to high jumps,

he's the best reindeer around!

Up last is graceful **Vixen**,

who's the **coolest** reindeer yet.

She ice-skates round the stadium, performing pirouettes.

The audience starts cheering
as confetti fills the skies.

Every reindeer **tried** their best,
but **who** will win the **prize?**

Santa gets the shining cup and smiles around with pride.

Who is the

Reindeer of the year?

It's **your** turn to decide!

THe enD